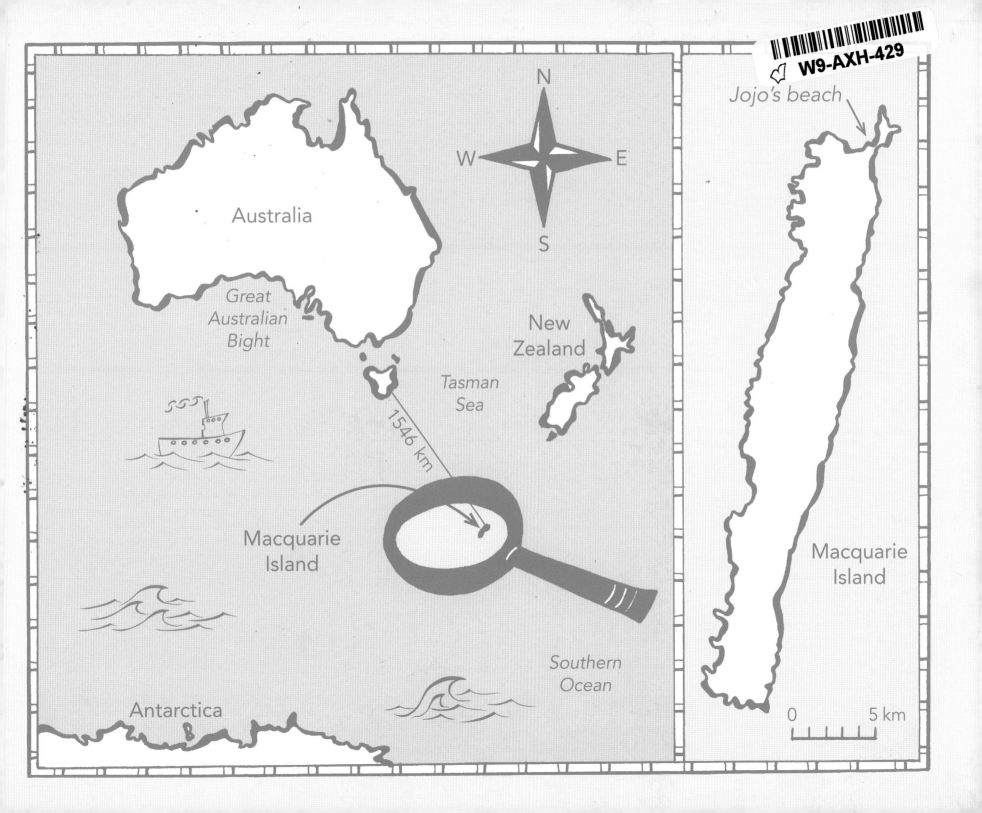

Australia

Great
Australian
Bight

N

W   E

S

New
Zealand

Tasman
Sea

1546 km

Macquarie
Island

Antarctica

Southern
Ocean

Jojo's beach

Macquarie
Island

0   5 km

For my Mum and Dad
Thanks for supporting me on every journey T.B.

For my Mummoo, Florence J.C.

A little penguin on a big swim

Tessa Bickford & Jennifer Castles

Photographs by Tessa Bickford

ALLEN&UNWIN

SYDNEY · MELBOURNE · AUCKLAND · LONDON

The first time I peeped out of my nest, this is what I saw.
My beautiful beach.

'If you keep swimming, Jojo, you'll reach the white snow land,'
says Daddoo. 'The icebergs are quite a sight to see.'

My little brother, Ballyhoo, likes to eat and sleep.

But I watch my beach all day long.
I can't wait to go to sea.

'Am I ready yet?' I ask.

'Not yet, little Jojo, not yet,' says Mummoo.
'You have to stay on the beach.'

Bubbah the elephant seal is sleeping on the soft moss.

On land he is a big, heavy blob,
but in the water he is fast and graceful.

Bubbah says the only thing better than
swimming in the sea is snoozing in the sun.

Hungry skua birds follow me home.

I shout at them, but then I have to run because their beaks are sharp and their eyes are glinty.

FLIPPA-FLAP, SNIPPA-SNAP, WADDLE-ODDLE-OOPS!

'Am I ready yet?' I ask.

'Not yet, little Jojo, not yet,' says Daddoo.
'You have to learn to swim.'

Penguin chicks hang around
the rock pools.

We tell stories about the orca. He's as
fast as a flash, with wicked pointy teeth.

'What would you do if he came after you?' says one chick.
'I would hide in the seaweed,' says the next chick.
'I would dive like a fish,' says another chick.
'I would bite him on the nose!' says me.

One day my fuzzy baby-coat starts to come off and there are smooth shiny feathers underneath.

Now when the skua bird swoops down I shout loud and puff out my belly.

FLIPPA-FLAP, SNIPPA-SNAP, SHOO-YOU-BOO!

I'm too big for her.

Every day I practise and now I can swim across
the biggest rock pool.

'Am I ready yet?' I ask.
'Yes you are, little Jojo,' says Mummoo.
'Take care, little Jojo,' says Daddoo.

'Bring me back a fish,'
says Ballyhoo.

At last …

First I swim through the seaweed forest;
all sticky arms and curly tails.

On the other side it's deep and clear, and there ahead is a field of
fish, a swirl of fish – more fish than I have ever seen!

I get busy. Loop-the-loop, SNAP goes one.
Zip-and-roll, SNAP goes two…

Suddenly the fish are gone
and the world goes dark.
A big, black shadow has crept up close.
Big like an ORCA.

It's too late to hide in the seaweed.
It's too late to dive like a fish.
It's too late to bite him on the nose.

FLIPPA-FLAP, SNIPPA-SNAP, OH JOJO NO!

His monster eye winks at me!

No sharp teeth, no fast as a flash…
that's not an orca!

The giant, gentle minke whale slides
right by and away into the blue.

I've had enough. I need to go back to my beautiful beach.

Back to Mummoo and Daddoo and Ballyhoo.
With a bellyful of fishlings and such a story to tell.

Tomorrow I'll swim further.

And one day I'll go as far as the white snow land.
I've heard the icebergs are quite a sight to see.

Now I'm ready for anything.

FLIPPA-FLAP, SNIPPA-SNAP, GO JOJO GO!

In 2008 I was offered the opportunity of a lifetime: to work as a fur seal researcher on one of the world's most remote sub-antarctic islands. After sailing through the fierce Southern Ocean for three days aboard the Australian research ship *Aurora Australis*, I arrived at Macquarie Island, my new home!

For six months I lived on this small island, studying the breeding and population growth of three types of fur seals. Every day I hiked to the island's busiest beaches, where I would count seals, catch and tag newborn pups, and collect DNA samples to help monitor their growth rate.

During the summer I also watched penguins, albatrosses and petrels throughout their breeding, hatching and feeding stages. Gentoo penguins usually hatch two babies in their grass nest by the beach. As the chicks begin to grow, they become adventurous and splash around in the shallow rock pools, their first attempt at swimming in the sea. There were many different characters among the seals and penguins. Some were bold, others were shy, and some were just lazy.

In the past the seals and penguins on Macquarie Island were hunted, but today they can breed there in safety. Around three-and-a-half million penguins and seabirds, and thousands of seals, use these beaches as their breeding ground each year. It was so inspiring to be close to these animals that I returned to Macquarie Island for another summer. I hope this book gives you a taste of what it is like to be there.

First published in 2012

Allen & Unwin
83 Alexander Street
Crows Nest NSW 2065
Australia
Phone: (61 2) 8425 0100
Fax: (61 2) 9906 2218
Email: info@allenandunwin.com
Web: www.allenandunwin.com

A Cataloguing-in-Publication entry is available from
the National Library of Australia
www.trove.nla.gov.au

ISBN 978 1 74331 017 5

Cover and text design by Sandra Nobes
Set in Avenir by Tou-Can Design
Front cover photograph by Krys Bailey, Marmotta PhotoArt, Photographers Direct
Photograph of baitfish on page 23 and author photograph on page 32 courtesy Dean Miller
Photographs of the minke whales on pages 24–25 and page 27 courtesy J Rumney,
'Swim with Whales' www.marineencounters.com.au
This book was printed in March 2012 at TWP SDN BHD, TAMPOI, No. 89 Jalan Tampoi,
Kawasan Perindustrian Tampoi, 80350 Johor Bahru

1 3 5 7 9 10 8 6 4 2

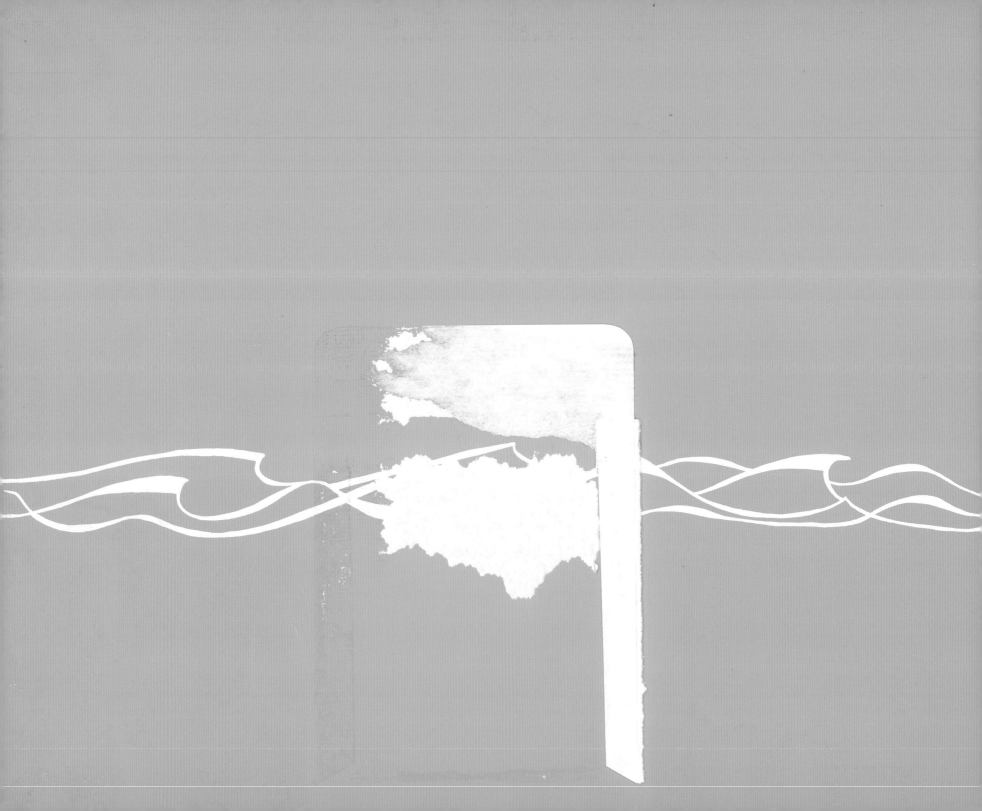